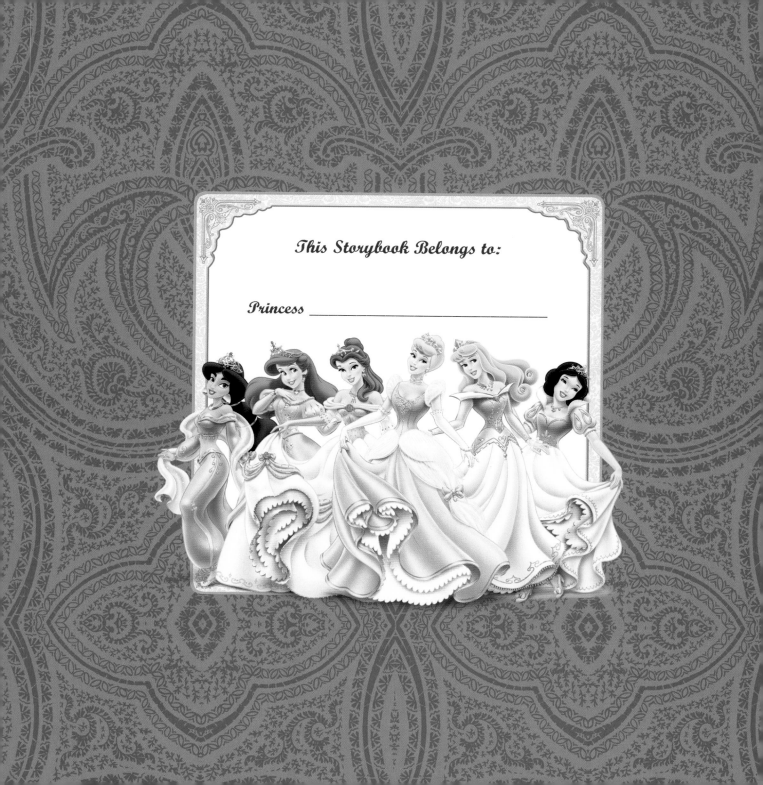

This Storybook Belongs to:

Princess _____

ADVANCE PUBLISHERS

Once upon a time, in the ancient city of Agrabah, there lived a young man named Aladdin. He was so very poor; he often had to steal food from the marketplace.

But Aladdin was determined not to remain a thief forever. "One day, Abu," he promised his pet monkey, "things will be different. We'll live in a palace and wear fine clothes, not rags."

Meanwhile, in the Sultan's luxurious palace, time was running out for the beautiful Princess Jasmine.

"The law says you must marry a prince before your next birthday," the Sultan said. "There are only three days left for you to choose a husband."

"The law is wrong!" cried Jasmine. "I don't want to marry anyone I do not love—even if he is a prince."

Jasmine ran tearfully into the gardens and hugged her pet tiger. "Oh, Rajah," she said. "I don't want to be a princess anymore." Then she planned her escape.

Early the next morning, the princess disguised herself in a long cloak and climbed over the palace walls.

Jasmine made her way through the busy marketplace. Seeing a hungry child, she picked up an apple from a stall and gave it to him. The princess did not know that she had to pay the fruit seller.

"Stop, thief!" shouted the man, running to grab the princess.

But Aladdin, who happened to overhear, jumped to Jasmine's rescue. He led her to the rooftop where he and Abu lived. As he gazed at the beautiful young girl, he knew he was falling in love.

Suddenly, the royal guards arrived and arrested Aladdin.

"Release him, by order of the princess!" Jasmine cried, pulling back her cloak.

"I would, Your Highness," said the chief guard who was surprised to see her. "But my orders come from Jafar."

Then the guards dragged Aladdin off to the palace dungeon.

Now, Jafar was the Sultan's most trusted adviser. But, unknown to the Sultan, he was plotting to take over the throne. Jafar knew of a magic lamp that would give him the power he needed, but it was hidden in the desert deep inside the Cave of Wonders.

The tiger head that guarded the Cave had told Jafar that only a "Diamond in the Rough" could enter—someone whose worth was hidden deep within.

Using his sorcery, Jafar discovered that this "Diamond in the Rough" was none other than Aladdin. So, disguised as an old beggar, Jafar freed Aladdin from the dungeon and led him through the desert.

Promising great wealth, Jafar persuaded Aladdin to enter the Cave and get the lamp for him. The fearsome tiger head warned them to touch nothing but the lamp.

Inside the first chamber, Aladdin and Abu met a friendly Magic Carpet who showed them where to find the lamp. But just as Aladdin picked it up, Abu caught sight of a magnificent jewel.

Forgetting the warning, Abu quickly snatched up the jewel. At that very moment, the walls of the Cave began to collapse and the floor gave way. Aladdin, Abu, and the Magic Carpet were trapped.

When the destruction had stopped, Aladdin studied the lamp. "What's so special about this dusty old thing?" he wondered, rubbing the dust away.

Suddenly, the lamp started to glow. A cloud of smoke billowed from its spout and became an enormous blue shape.

"I am your Genie, direct from the lamp," said the creature. To prove his powers, he got Aladdin and his friends out of the Cave and offered him three wishes.

Aladdin thought of Princess Jasmine. She would never marry a poor street boy. "Genie," he said, "I wish to be a prince."

The Genie waved his hand and turned Aladdin into a prince. Abu became a magnificent elephant that would carry Aladdin into Agrabah.

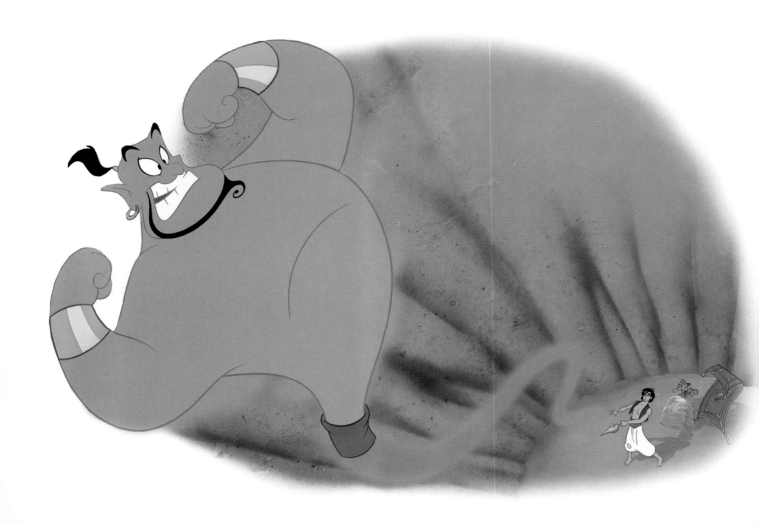

Calling himself Prince Ali Ababwa, Aladdin marched towards the Sultan's palace in a grand procession.

That night, Aladdin took Princess Jasmine for a moonlit ride on the Magic Carpet. When they returned, Jasmine knew that Prince Ali was really Aladdin. She had found a prince she wanted to marry.

But Jafar had other plans for Prince Ali. He ordered his guards to capture the prince and throw him into the sea.

As Aladdin sank beneath the waves, the lamp fell from his turban. Using Aladdin's second wish, the Genie saved his master from drowning.

Back at the palace, the wicked Jafar had hypnotized the Sultan using his magic staff. "You will marry Jafar," the Sultan ordered Jasmine.

"Never!" cried Jasmine. "Father, what's wrong with you?"

"I know!" said Aladdin, bursting into the room.

He snatched the staff from Jafar and smashed it to pieces. At once, the Sultan snapped out of his trance.

Jafar fled. But, as he left, he glimpsed the magic lamp peeking out from Aladdin's turban.

"So," thought Jafar, hiding safely in the tower, "Prince Ali is really that ragged street urchin, Aladdin—and he has the lamp. But not for long!"

The next morning, Jafar's cunning parrot, Iago, flew silently into Aladdin's room and stole the lamp.

"At last!" Jafar cried. "I am your master now!" He rubbed the lamp and watched the Genie appear.

Reluctantly, the Genie obeyed Jafar's orders and made him the Sultan. Then, Jafar wished to be the most powerful sorcerer in the world.

Jafar sent Aladdin, Abu, and the Magic Carpet to the other side of the world. Then, he cast a spell over the palace. He suspended Jasmine's father from the ceiling like a puppet while Jasmine became his servant.

Finally, when Aladdin returned to the palace—thanks to the Magic Carpet—Jafar turned his attention to him.

Aladdin bravely took up a sword and challenged Jafar to a fight. In reply, the evil sorcerer conjured up a flaming wall of fire and turned himself into a huge, terrifying cobra.

Jafar raised his head to strike Aladdin. "Did you think you could beat the most powerful being on Earth?" he snarled.

Aladdin thought quickly of a way to trick Jafar. "The Genie has much more power than you!" he teased.

The power-mad sorcerer knew that Aladdin was right. "Genie," he said, "my final wish is to be the most powerful genie of all."

A swirling mist of light surrounded Jafar, and he changed shape once again. Then, to his own amazement, Jafar and Iago were sucked into a lamp. Like all genies, Jafar was now trapped forever. He was a prisoner inside the lamp. The evil spell was broken.

"Jasmine, I'm sorry I lied to you," said Aladdin. "I'm not a prince at all—I'm only the poor street boy you met in the market."

The Genie appeared at Aladdin's side. "You still have your third wish left, Al," he said. "I can make you a prince again."

But Aladdin wished for the Genie's freedom instead.

"You'll always be a prince to me," the Genie told him.

"That's right," the Sultan agreed. "You've proved your worth as far as I'm concerned. What we need is a new law. I decree that from this day, the princess may marry whomever she chooses!"

"I choose Aladdin!" Jasmine cried.

At last, the princess had found the prince of her dreams. All of Agrabah looked forward to their wedding day...and to Jasmine and Aladdin living happily ever after.